You forgot your Skirt, Amelia Bloomer!

A Very Improper Story

by
Shana Corey

illustrated by
Chesley McLaren

Scholastic Press   New York

Library of Congress catalog card number: 99-27181

ISBN:0-439-07819-9

10 9 8 7 6 5 4 3 2 1   0/0 01 02 03 04 05

Printed in Singapore   46

First edition, March 2000

The illustrations in this book were painted in gouache.

The display type was hand lettered by Chesley McLaren.

The text type was set in Countryhouse.

Book design by Marijka Kostiw

To everyone I know and love, and most especially to Pio Alberto;

my parents, Beverly and Michael Corey;

and my sister, Marci Corey (one of the most improper women I know).

With giant armfuls of thanks to Tracy Mack

and Heidi Kilgras for making this possible.

— S. C.

To all those who dare to be IMPROPER!

Special thanks to Tracy Mack and Marijka Kostiw

for making my first book such a wonderful experience.

— C. M.

Amelia Bloomer
was NOT a proper lady.

In fact, Amelia Bloomer thought proper ladies were silly.

She thought it was silly that proper ladies
were not allowed to vote. So she tried
to change the laws so that they could.

"Good grief," people said.

Amelia Bloomer thought it was silly that proper ladies were not supposed to work. So she started her own newspaper and went to work on that.

LILY.

OF WOMEN. VOL. 3

MARCH 1851.

TO DO—
1 WOMEN
VOTE
WORK

She named the newspaper THE LILY. It was a special newspaper all about women. She hired other women to work on it, too.

THE LILY
DEVOTED TO THE INTERESTS OF WOMEN

WORK? WHY WORK?"

"A shame," people said.

But the silliest thing of all, thought Amelia Bloomer, was the way proper ladies were supposed to dress. Their dresses were so heavy, wearing them was like carting around . . .

. . . a dozen bricks!

What was proper about that?

Their dresses were so long that proper ladies looked like walking broomsticks. They acted like broomsticks, too, because their skirts swept up all the mud and trash from the street.

What was proper about that?

The corsets they wore underneath their dresses were so tight it was hard
to breathe in them. Proper ladies were fainting at the drop of a hat.

What was proper about that?

And the hoops they wore beneath their dresses were so wide that
no matter how they squeezed, no matter how they squished and squashed
and stuffed themselves through, proper ladies still got stuck in doorways all over town.

What in the world was proper about that?

Even little girls had to wear proper dresses.
So they couldn't run or jump or play.

"This has got to stop!" declared Amelia Bloomer.

Then one day, Amelia's friend Elizabeth Cady Stanton came to visit.
Elizabeth brought her cousin Libby with her. Libby looked remarkable!

She was even more improper than Amelia because

Libby was not wearing a dress!

"Dresses," said Libby. "Bah! How silly!"

Instead of a dress, Libby was wearing something
that was NOT too heavy and NOT too long and
NOT too tight and NOT too wide. It looked just right.

"Brilliant!" announced Amelia.

FRONT LEG A

CUT 2.

BACK LEG A

CUT 2.

And she went right
to her sewing machine
and sewed
a matching outfit
for herself.

Then she went out for a walk.

The townspeople were aghast.

"You forgot your skirt,
Amelia Bloomer!" called a little boy.

"Shocking!" everyone said.

But Amelia
didn't care
one bit.
She thought
the new clothes
were
wonderful!

She ran

and jumped

and twirled . . .

...and did

all the things

she had always

wanted to do.

Amelia had such a good time that she wanted other women to know about the new clothes, too. So when she got home, she wrote about them in THE LILY.

"Marvelous!" said a lady from Boston.

"I declare!" said a lady from Charleston.

"Where can I get one?" asked a lady from Baltimore.

Pretty soon Amelia had letters from women everywhere.

They all wanted patterns so they could make the new clothes themselves.

Some of them even wanted tips on what to wear with the new style.

Some people called the new style of clothes the American Costume.

Most people just called them Bloomers.

Of course, not EVERYONE liked Bloomers.

"Hmmph," said one very proper gentleman.

"Balderdash," said another.

"This can only lead to more rights for women," grumbled a third.

1920's Swimwear

60's bellbottoms

80's Power Suit

Over time, Bloomers went out of style. Proper ladies and gentlemen everywhere breathed a sigh of relief.

"Thank goodness," they said. "Now everyone will forget this nonsense and things can return to **normal**."

But did people really forget all about Amelia Bloomer and her improper ideas?

Well . . .

. . . what do you think?

AMELIA JENKS BLOOMER was born in Homer, New York, in 1818. She worked as a governess and a teacher before marrying Dexter Bloomer, a Quaker newspaper editor from Seneca Falls, New York, where the couple settled in 1840.

In 1847, the course of Amelia's life – and history – changed forever when Elizabeth Cady Stanton, one of the most prominent spokespeople for women's rights, moved to town. Seneca Falls soon became the center of the American women's movement, and in 1848 hosted the first women's rights convention.

Inspired by the convention, a Ladies' Temperance Society was formed, with Amelia serving as an officer. On January 1, 1849, a newspaper called THE LILY was launched in order to give the society a mouthpiece. It was the first newspaper to be edited entirely by a woman. Amelia was the editor.

Amelia was never one to stay quiet when she saw wrongdoing, and so it wasn't long before editorials on women's rights began appearing in THE LILY alongside the articles against drink. The issue that made THE LILY famous was dress reform.

Women's clothing at the time was very restrictive and weighed between 20 and 40 pounds! On even the hottest days, women wore layers upon layers of petticoats – some of them flannel – under their long skirts. The petticoats made skirts stick out so far that between 20 to 30 yards of material was needed to make the top skirt! Narrow waists were in fashion, and the wider the skirt, the smaller the waist was thought to look.

Tightly laced corsets, supported by whalebone and sometimes steel, were also worn to make waists look small. Corsets made it impossible for women to move their arms freely and were so tight that they caused difficulty breathing and digesting and actually displaced internal organs! The fashion was uncomfortable and dangerous, but what were the other options? Amelia was about to make them known.

In the winter of 1850-1851, Elizabeth Cady Stanton's cousin Elizabeth "Libby" Miller came to visit Seneca Falls. She was wearing an unusual outfit consisting of baggy pantaloons with a short skirt over them. Libby had seen the attire in Europe, worn by women recuperating from health problems. She adapted it as a traveling outfit for herself on her honeymoon. She was still wearing the style when she visited Seneca Falls.

Amelia loved the outfit and printed an article about it in THE LILY urging women to adopt it. The article was picked up by newspapers nationwide and the circulation of THE LILY doubled almost overnight.

Reformers such as Stanton and Susan B. Anthony quickly began wearing the new clothes, as did many female athletes. But though many women loved the costume, there was also considerable resistance to it. Some people thought the clothes were unwomanly, and they mocked them and their wearers. Cartoons, popular songs, and even theater productions openly made fun of the costume. Opponents of women's rights began equating the movement with the costume and started calling reformers "Bloomers," too. After a few years, Amelia and the other reformers stopped wearing bloomers because they didn't want the entire movement reduced to a battle over clothing.

Amelia Bloomer eventually moved to the Iowa frontier with her husband and adopted two children. She never stopped working for women's rights.

Bloomers went on to be worn in various styles, with the name becoming representative of independent thinking – just the kind of quality that Amelia herself was known for. From 1890 to 1920 there was even a women's baseball league called the Bloomer League. And to this day, the name "bloomer" is still in use.

Today women and girls can wear whatever they want. Perhaps it wouldn't be that way, though, if all those years ago Amelia Bloomer hadn't had the courage to be "improper" and to take a stand for something she believed in.

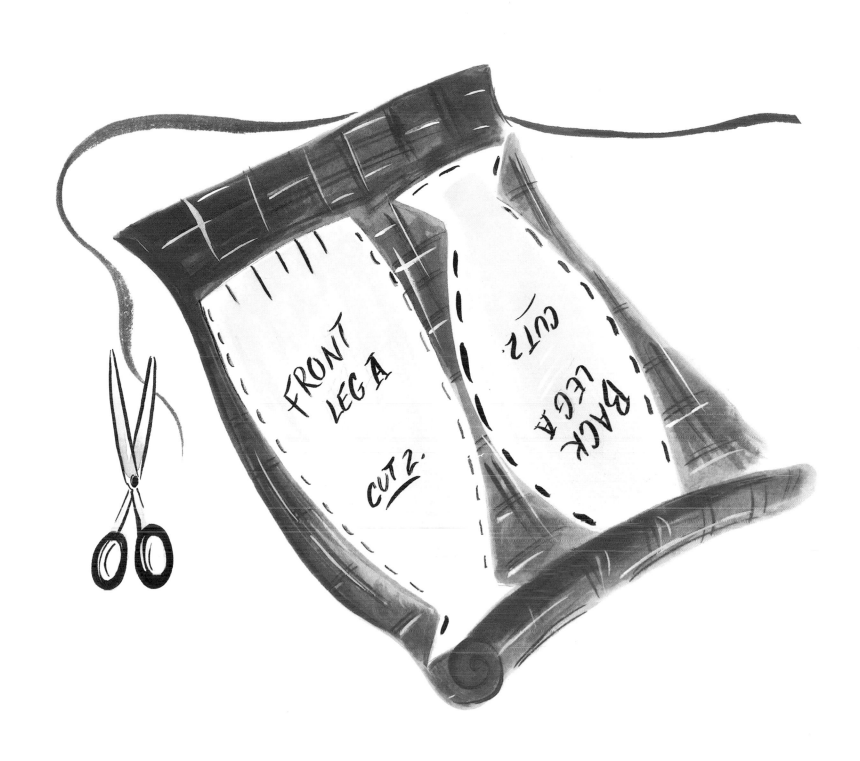

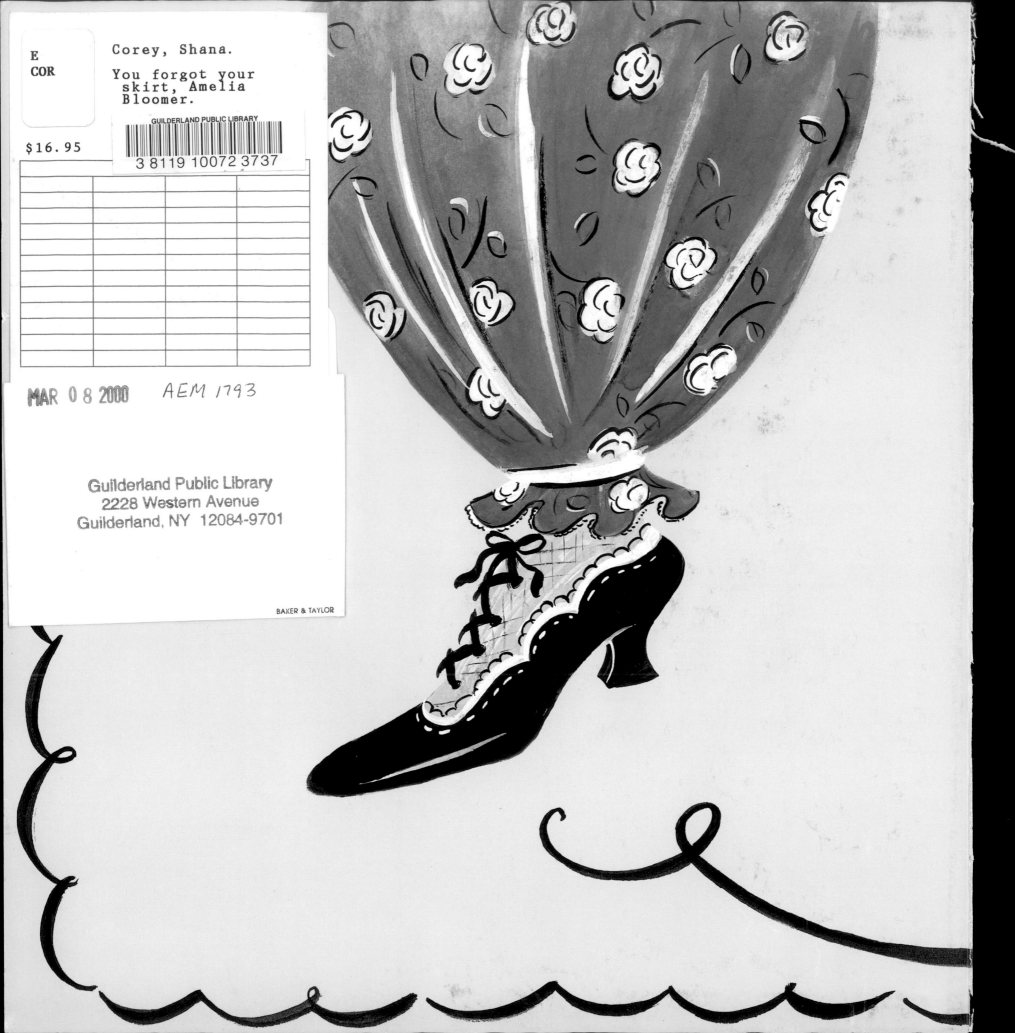